To Adele and Emily

DINOSAUR CHASE!
A HUTCHINSON BOOK 0 0918 9293 7

Published in Great Britain by Hutchinson,
an imprint of Random House Children's Books

This edition published 2006

1 3 5 7 9 10 8 6 4 2

RANDOM HOUSE CHILDREN'S BOOKS
61–63 Uxbridge Road, London W5 5SA
A division of The Random House Group Ltd

RANDOM HOUSE AUSTRALIA (PTY) LTD
20 Alfred Street, Milsons Point, Sydney,
New South Wales 2061, Australia

RANDOM HOUSE NEW ZEALAND LTD
18 Poland Road, Glenfield, Auckland 10, New Zealand

RANDOM HOUSE (PTY) LTD
Endulini, 5A Jubilee Road, Parktown 2193, South Africa

THE RANDOM HOUSE GROUP Limited Reg. No. 954009
www.kidsatrandomhouse.co.uk

A CIP catalogue record for this book is available from the British Library.

Printed in Singapore

Dinosaur Chase!

Benedict Blathwayt

HUTCHINSON

London   Sydney   Auckland   Johannesburg

Fin and his friends were playing games.
"Watch this!" shouted Fin.
"That's easy," yelled another dinosaur.
"I can do that!"

"Bet you can't do this!"

"Or this!"

"How about this!"

"Or even THIS...!"

Just then a gang of bullies turned up.
But they were too rough and
they spoilt the game.
"Hey!" cried Fin.
"You can't do that!"

"Oh yes we can!" said the biggest of the bullies.
"We can do whatever WE want. And what can YOU
do about it, with your spindly legs, knobbly
ankles and bony tail? And look at those
spiky claws and feeble FLUFFY arms!"

Fin's friends could see it was time to run away.

So Fin ran too.
And his spindly legs went very fast . . .

But the bullies could all run as fast as Fin.
"We can do that," they jeered.

So Fin jumped and his knobbly ankles sprang him high over a fallen tree.

One of the bullies couldn't jump...

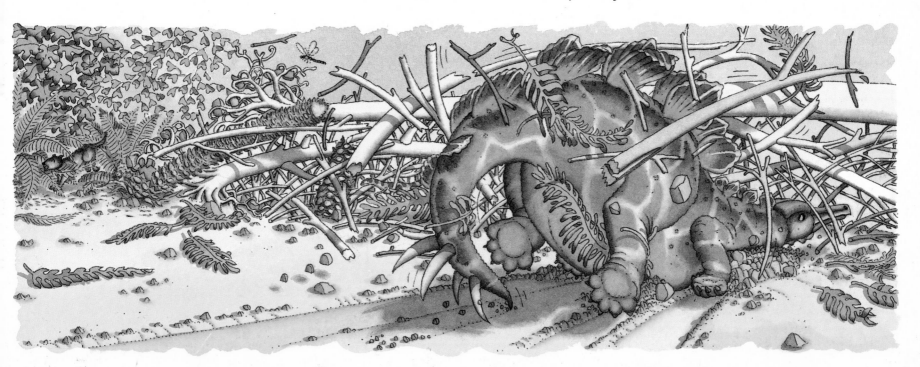

But the rest of them could.
"We can do that," they shouted.
"We can jump too!"

So Fin dived into the lagoon.

And his bony tail swished him through
the water at great speed.
One of the bullies couldn't swim...

But the other two were strong swimmers.
"We can do that," they yelled.
"We can swim too!"

So when Fin reached the other side, he ducked behind
a boulder and hid. He stayed very still, and very quiet,
until he felt sure it was safe to come out...

"BOO!"

The other dinosaurs jumped out.
"We can do that!" they laughed.
"We can hide too!"

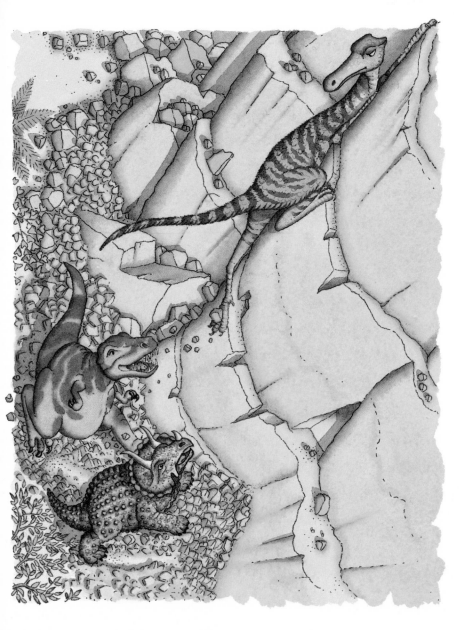

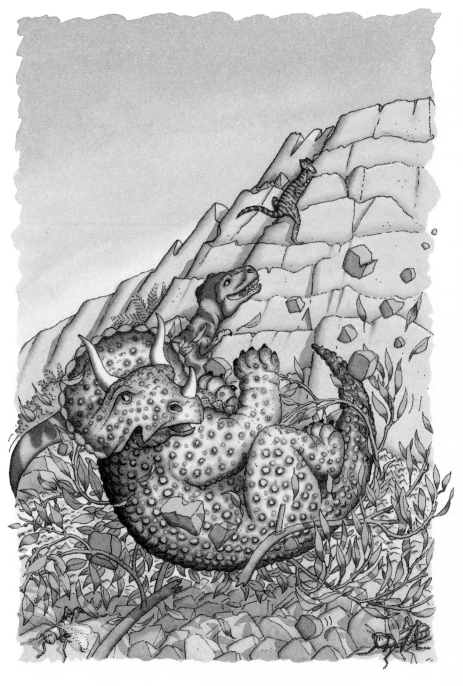

So Fin began to climb.
And his spiky claws helped him
up the steep, rough rock face.

One of the bullies couldn't climb…

But the biggest, meanest,
fiercest one could.
"I can do that," he sneered.
"I can climb too!"

So Fin ran faster and faster and faster, and when
he reached the top he just could not stop…

"Help!" cried Fin as he tumbled off the mountain. But he spread out his arms and his wonderful **feathers** stretched tight in the wind.

"I can't do THAT!" roared the biggest, meanest, fiercest dinosaur of them all. And he stamped his enormous feet and swished his heavy tail until the whole mountain shook.

"I can!" cried Fin. "Look at me . . .

I can fly!"

And Fin soared through the air,
free as a bird, far above the ground.